LITTLE GREY RABBIT
AND THE WEASELS

LITTLE GREY RABBIT AND THE WEASELS

By Alison Uttley
Pictures by Margaret Tempest

templar publishing

DOWN IN THE DELL lived a family of Weasels. They had a dark little house, built against a wall where nobody could see it. The door was hidden behind a curtain of foxglove leaves, and the foxglove bells rang when anybody passed. The narrow windows were covered with moss, and in the middle of each there was a tiny crack where the Weasels peeped out.

"There goes Milkman Hedgehog," they cried, as Old Hedgehog walked slowly past.

Then one of them would run as softly as a shadow after him, and dip a mug in the can of milk without Hedgehog knowing.

One day, Speckledy Hen was strolling that way with a basket of eggs for Little Grey Rabbit. It was a sunny day and she sang a little clucking song as she went along the narrow path:

Clucketty, Clucketty, Cluck.
My eggs will bring good luck.
Little Grey Rabbit, and Squirrel and Hare,
Will each have one and one to spare.
Clucketty, Clucketty, Cluck.

She passed close to the Weasels' house,
but she did not know it was there. She did not
see the sharp eyes watching her, or hear the
whispers behind the mossy windows.

"Three brown eggs and one to spare. How
many is that?" asked William Weasel.

"Five eggs," said Winkie
Weasel.

"No, it's four,"
said Winnie Weasel,
who had once been
to school for a day.

"Be quick and get
them," whispered
William.

Out they slipped and away after the Speckledy Hen. They stole the eggs from under the white cloth, and carried them home.

The little Hen walked on, knowing nothing.

She stepped daintily through the daisies, up to Grey Rabbit's house, tapped on the door with her beak and popped her head inside.

"Oh, my dear Speckledy Hen! How glad I am to see you!" cried Grey Rabbit.

"Dear Grey Rabbit! This is a pleasure!" said the Speckledy Hen, and she fanned herself with her bonnet. "My! It is hot."

"Take a seat, dear Speckledy," said Grey Rabbit, drawing forward the rocking chair.

"Thank you, Grey Rabbit. I've never perched on a swinging chair before," said the Speckledy Hen, swaying to and fro.

"Hare likes rocking too," laughed Grey Rabbit. "Here he comes," she added as Hare came bouncing in, followed by Squirrel.

"Hallo, Speckledy Hen!" cried Hare.

"Welcome," said Squirrel, shaking the Hen's wing.

"Have you brought something in that basket?" asked Hare. "A present or something?"

"Oh, Hare! Hush!" whispered Grey Rabbit.

Speckledy Hen smiled. "Do you like eggs, Hare?" she asked.

"I do! We all do!" replied Hare, licking his lips.

"Well, look in my basket!" said she.

Hare twitched the snowy cloth from the basket.

"Oh, it's empty!" he cried.

The Speckledy Hen flew out of the chair and stared into the basket.

"I put in one egg for Hare and one for Squirrel and two for Grey Rabbit," said she.

"Four eggs, all gone!" cried Grey Rabbit.

"Did you leave the basket anywhere?" asked Squirrel.

The Speckledy Hen shook her little head.

"A master thief," said Hare.

"A magical trick," said Squirrel.

They gave the Speckledy Hen a glass of wine and a cake, and they talked of eggs and eggs.

Then Grey Rabbit filled the basket with lettuces and herbs.

"I'll go home another way," said Speckledy Hen.

Another day, Moldy Warp the Mole was walking down the lane. He carried his little axe over his shoulder.

"I'll cut a nice branch from an elder tree and make a whistle," said he to himself. "Then I'll play a tune outside Grey Rabbit's window and give her a surprise."

He went slowly past the Weasels' house, and he looked up at the fine foxglove growing there. He saw nothing of the fierce eyes watching him.

"Here's a big foxglove. I could cut it down if I wanted," he thought, and he leaned his axe against the foxglove stem.

He did not see the skinny paw that snatched the axe away.

Moldy Warp fumbled in his pocket for his pipe, and as he searched for it he hummed a tune.

This is what he hummed:

Hum-mm, it's a very nice day.
Hum-mm, I'm going to play.
Hum-mm, on my whistle tonight,
Hum-mm, for Grey Rabbit's delight.

He struck a light and puffed at the lavender tobacco.

Somebody snatched the pipe from his lips, and before he could turn round, another Weasel dragged his waistcoat over his head.

"Help! Help! Robbers! Thieves!" shouted Mole. The waistcoat came off, and Mole was left staring about.

"Was it the wind?" he cried. "I heard nobody, I saw nobody, but somebody took my waistcoat. Who was it?"

He trotted quickly along to Grey Rabbit's house and told his story.

"Poor old Moldy Warp!" said Grey Rabbit,
wrapping a rug round him. "I'll make you a
new waistcoat tonight."

"Poor old Moldy Warp," said Hare. "I'll give you my axe."

"Poor old Moldy Warp!" said Squirrel. "I'll make you a briar pipe."

Mole sat in the rocking chair, shaking his head.

"It's very kind of you, my friends, and I thank you very much, but what I want to know is, how did my pipe and axe and waistcoat go? They vanished. They flew!"

"Wings," said Hare. "They got wings."

"Speckledy Hen lost her eggs," said Grey Rabbit.

"Hedgehog lost his milk," said Squirrel.

"There's some mystery in the little lane," said Hare. "Let's call it Shady Lane."

"Stay here tonight, Moldy Warp," begged Little Grey Rabbit. "I'll put a bed in the kitchen for you."

Moldy Warp was delighted. He had never slept in the little house.

Grey Rabbit cut out a little woollen waistcoat and stitched it with scarlet thread. Squirrel made a briar pipe and filled it with dried lavender from the bunch hanging near the fire. Hare sat and talked and told all his old tales.

It was indeed a merry evening, and when the moon came out Grey Rabbit put a couple of blankets on the floor and a little pillow stuffed with feathers for Moldy Warp.

Then they said goodnight, and went upstairs to bed. The stars and moon shone in at the window as Moldy Warp lay down on the hearthrug by Grey Rabbit's fire.

"Gr-gr-gr," the snores came from Hare's
room.

"Too-whit, too-whoo," called Wise Owl,
flying over the roof.

Mole looked at the nice new waistcoat Grey Rabbit had made, which hung on a chair nearby. Then he lay down and fell fast asleep.

The Weasels were enjoying themselves in their secret house. They crept out at night and got plenty to eat. During the day they robbed anyone who went by. Robin, the postman, lost his mailbag, Water Rat lost his frills one afternoon and Fuzzypeg lost his lesson bag with all his homework.

"I don't really mind," he confessed. "I couldn't do the sums."

Only Wise Owl and Grey Rabbit had not been troubled. Squirrel had the green bow nipped off her tail, and Hare had his watch stolen.

"I ran like the wind, or my coat would've gone from my back," he cried when he got home.

"You mustn't go down Shady Lane, Grey Rabbit. It isn't safe."

Grey Rabbit didn't want to go down Shady Lane. She thought she might lose her little blue apron.

Then, one day, she was late coming home from market, and she took the short cut past the tall foxgloves where the Weasels' house was hidden.

Her little basket was filled with good things. There was barley sugar for Hare, a loaf of honey bread and a piece of cloth to make Squirrel a dress.

Grey Rabbit hurried along the lane, holding her basket tight, looking here and there, keeping a watch for robbers.

She was rather frightened, so she sang a little song to keep herself brave:

The sun and the moon
came down one day,
To live in the animals' wood.
They kept them safe, and drove away
The wicked and helped the good.

The Weasels were watching from their mossy windows.

"Hush! Hush!" they whispered. "We'll catch her, basket and all." They crept down to the door and looked outside.

The little Rabbit was singing as she came past.

Suddenly William Weasel snatched her basket, and Winkie and Winnie leapt from the leaves.

They swept her quickly through the door into the house.

"Oh, dear me! Oh, dear!" cried Grey Rabbit. "Please let me go home."

"No, Grey Rabbit! We've been waiting for you," said the Weasels, chuckling. "We want somebody to bake and wash and clean."

"Please, I have to go home," said Grey Rabbit. "Squirrel and Hare can't do without me."

"They must. Here you are, and here you will stay. Nobody will find you."

So Grey Rabbit knew she must make the best of it. She cooked for the fierce Weasels, and cleaned their little house. She polished the rusty saucepans and washed the clothes. She worked all day.

At night she slept in one of the little
bedrooms. The stars shone through the tiny
crack in the window and the wind blew under
the door.

Downstairs the Weasels were laughing and clinking their glasses. They were rejoicing they had caught Grey Rabbit.

Hare and Squirrel searched everywhere for their friend. Hare even ventured to Wise Owl's tree and rang the bell.

"Grey Rabbit gone?" hooted Wise Owl. "Very careless of you, Hare. Go home and find her."

Poor Hare turned sadly away, and Wise Owl called him back.

"I'll help you, Hare. You look by day and I'll hunt by night."

Hare ventured down Shady Lane, looking for Grey Rabbit's basket.

He passed the Weasels' house, but there was no sound or sight of anyone. Then out darted a Weasel and grabbed Hare's clean handkerchief, which he had taken to wave as a truce to Wise Owl. Hare scurried home in a fright.

Grey Rabbit saw the handkerchief, with the letter H in the corner. "Poor old Hare," she thought, sadly. "His Sunday hanky."

That night, the Weasels fetched her to the kitchen where they sat round the fire.

"Sing to us, Grey Rabbit," they commanded.

"I'll sing if you promise not to hurt my friends, or take their things," said Grey Rabbit. "I won't sing a note unless you promise."

"We promise," said the Weasels at last.

So Grey Rabbit straightened her apron, raised her brave little head and sang to the Weasels. First she sang, "a frog he would a-wooing go," and the Weasels clapped and asked for more.

Grey Rabbit sang them many a song.

How the Weasels clapped and stamped and shouted "Hurrah!" as they tried to join in the choruses.

Wise Owl was flying slowly down Shady Lane, listening to the rustle of leaves and flowers.

"What's that noise?" he asked himself.

He flew down on his silent wings and waited there. He could hear the stamping and squeaking.

Then he heard a well-known little
voice singing.

He flew close and put one eye to the mossy window. He could just see inside the room. A candle was burning on the table, the Weasels sat around and Grey Rabbit was singing.

"Too-whit, too-whoo," called Wise Owl loudly, and the candle was blown out and the Weasels were quiet.

"Hush! Go to bed, Grey Rabbit. There's that pesky Owl flying over," said they.

So Grey Rabbit went up the crooked stair to her room. She pressed her face to the window crack, and Wise Owl saw her.

"Oh, Wise Owl! Save me!" she whispered, and she opened the window. Wise Owl broke away the moss, and balanced on the sill.

Grey Rabbit climbed on his back and clung to his feathers. Away he flew, but the tip of his wing caught the foxglove and set all the bells ringing.

"What's that? The bells ringing an alarm!" cried the Weasels. They were too late. Wise Owl and Grey Rabbit had gone.

Wise Owl dropped her gently on her own doorstep, and then he flew off.

"Hare! Squirrel! Here I am! Let me in!" called Grey Rabbit, banging at the door. Hare and Squirrel came tumbling downstairs, half asleep.

"Grey Rabbit! Where have you been? How did you get home?" they asked, as they brought her in and locked the door again.

"Wise Owl saved me!" said Grey Rabbit. "He did! He did! I flew on his back."

"On the Owl's back?" echoed Hare and Squirrel.

Now, Wise Owl had flown away to the Weasels' house. He shook the door and shouted to them.

"Ho, all you Weasel tribe!" said he. "Pack up your belongings and depart at once. If you are here tomorrow I shall make a meal of you. Take warning, and you must leave behind everything you stole."

The Weasels packed their little cart with their pots and pans and chairs and bedding.

"Don't forget Mole's waistcoat, and Hare's handkerchief, and the axe, and the schoolbag," they said. "Let's go away before anyone is awake."

Wise Owl flew over just as they were starting.

"Have you left the stolen goods?" he asked.
So the Weasels had to take off all the
treasures they had thieved. Away they went,
as cross as three cross sticks.

The next day Grey Rabbit set off with a basket of presents for Wise Owl.

She rang the little bell at his doorway.

"Who's that?" yawned Wise Owl. "Oh, it's you, Grey Rabbit. I'm glad you are none the worse for your flight."

"It was lovely!" cried Grey Rabbit. "I knew Hare or Squirrel or Moldy Warp or Hedgehog or Fuzzypeg or you would save me. I'm glad it was you, Wise Owl. I liked flying high in the air. It was a great adventure, like going in an aeroplane."

"Yes, I am a kind of aeroplane," replied Wise Owl, and he flew back to his hole in the beech tree and fell asleep.

WHICH LITTLE GREY RABBIT BOOKS DO YOU HAVE?

A LITTLE GREY RABBIT BOOK

**THE SQUIRREL,
THE HARE AND THE
LITTLE GREY RABBIT**

By Alison Uttley
Pictures by Margaret Tempest

A LITTLE GREY RABBIT BOOK

**HOW
LITTLE GREY RABBIT
GOT BACK HER TAIL**

By Alison Uttley
Pictures by Margaret Tempest

A LITTLE GREY RABBIT BOOK

**SQUIRREL
GOES SKATING**

By Alison Uttley
Pictures by Margaret Tempest

A LITTLE GREY RABBIT BOOK

**LITTLE GREY RABBIT'S
CHRISTMAS**

By Alison Uttley
Pictures by Margaret Tempest

LITTLE GREY RABBIT'S VALENTINE

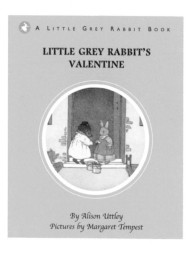

By Alison Uttley
Pictures by Margaret Tempest

HARE AND THE EASTER EGGS

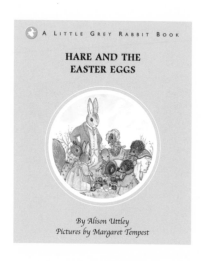

By Alison Uttley
Pictures by Margaret Tempest

LITTLE GREY RABBIT'S BIRTHDAY

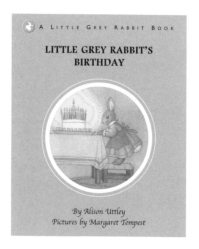

By Alison Uttley
Pictures by Margaret Tempest

THE STORY OF FUZZYPEG THE HEDGEHOG

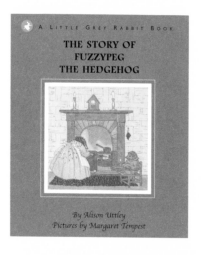

By Alison Uttley
Pictures by Margaret Tempest

A TEMPLAR BOOK

This edition first published in the UK in 2016 by Templar Publishing,
part of the Bonnier Publishing Group,
The Plaza, 535 King's Road, London, SW10 0SZ

www.templarco.co.uk
www.bonnierpublishing.com

Original edition first published in the UK in 1947
by William Collins Sons & Co Ltd

This edition edited by Susan Dickinson and Kitty Imbert
Additional design by Ellie Wahba

1 3 5 7 9 10 8 6 4 2

ISBN 978-1-78370-471-2

Printed in China